For Célia

The Loudest Roar

Thomas Taylor

OXFORD

UNIVERSITY PRESS

The jungle was a peaceful place.
Everyone was quiet. Everyone was calm.

Well, nearly everyone.

Clovis was a tiger.
Even though he was only small, he knew
he was the fiercest, most roaringest tiger
in the whole world.

And Clovis
thought that
everyone else
should know
it too.

One day, he saw some parrots
chatting politely as they
picked their juicy fruit.

ROAR!

Suddenly - there was Clovis!

He found some muddy wildebeest
wallowing happily in their slimy swamp.

They didn't see the roaringest tiger
in the whole world.

Then, suddenly - there was Clovis!

The mighty elephants
were sunning themselves
peacefully at
the edge of
the jungle.

But what could they do?
Then a monkey, who was
very clever, had an idea.

Clovis didn't notice

the others

creeping up

on him.

Then,
suddenly...

Clovis was
very surprised.

It was the
loudest
roar he had
ever heard.

The little monkey
looked up at the fiercest,
most roaringest tiger in the world.
'If you promise not to roar at us,' he said,
'then we promise not to roar at you.'
Clovis said he would try.

The jungle was a peaceful place.
Everyone was quiet. Everyone was calm.

And Clovis
was very well behaved . . .

. . . most of the time.

OXFORD

UNIVERSITY PRESS

Great Clarendon Street, Oxford OX2 6DP

Oxford University Press is a department of the University of Oxford.
It furthers the University's objective of excellence in research, scholarship,
and education by publishing worldwide in

Oxford   New York

Auckland   Cape Town   Dar es Salaam   Hong Kong   Karachi
Kuala Lumpur   Madrid   Melbourne   Mexico City   Nairobi
New Delhi   Shanghai   Taipei   Toronto

With offices in

Argentina   Austria   Brazil   Chile   Czech Republic   France   Greece
Guatemala   Hungary   Italy   Japan   Poland   Portugal   Singapore
South Korea   Switzerland   Thailand   Turkey   Ukraine   Vietnam

Oxford is a registered trade mark of Oxford University Press
in the UK and in certain other countries

British Library Cataloguing in Publication Data

Data available

ISBN-13: 978-0-19-272518-9 (paperback)
ISBN-10: 0-19-272518-1 (paperback)
ISBN-13: 978-0-19-271987-4 (paperback with audio CD)
ISBN-10: 0-19-271987-4 (paperback with audio CD)

7 9 10 8

Printed in China